The al

words by T.A.Z. Razzle
illustrated by Neil Curtis

a is for apple

b for big,

e for egg and

f for five,

g for gate and

h for hive.

i for in

j for jam,

k for key and

l for lamb.

m for moon

n for nurse

o for orange and

p for purse.

q for queen

r for rose,

s for sun and

t for toes.

u for up

v for vet,

W for water that makes us wet.

x says the angry cat,

y for you,

Z for zebra that we see in the zoo!